You can be anything!
Dream big!

Hayley Rose

www.fifothebear.com

FIFO
"When I Grow Up"

by Hayley Rose

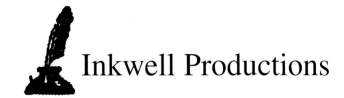
Inkwell Productions

Published By
INKWELL PRODUCTIONS
3370 N. Hayden Rd. # 123-276
Scottsdale, AZ 85251
Tel: 480-315-9636
Fax: 480-315-9641
Toll Free: 1-888-324-BOOK (2665)
Email: Info@InkwellProductions.com
Website: www.InkwellProductions.com

ISBN: 0-9718155-0-X

Library of Congress catalog control number: 2002108428

ACKNOWLEDGEMENTS

To my family,
Reba Rose, Melissa Rose, Sydney Powell, Evelyn Groman,
and to the Shein family, Cari, Barry, Rebecca and Megan,
for their love, encouragement and support.

To my extended family,
Laura, Greg and Zachary Zepkin,
Henry and Vicki Schiffer, Bonnie Link, and Andrea Link.
Thank you for taking me in and always believing in me.

To my friends,
Kari Berry, Sandy Downing, Arcturus Wicker, Kristine and
Edward Artinian, Helen Kim, Marquis Davis, Brooke Lampert, and
Bernie Lorenzo. You're the best!

To Nick – A true dream maker.
From start to finish he's there every step of the way,
helping you to put out the best book you possibly can.
He truly cares about the author and the art.
Thank you Nick, and the entire Inkwell staff.

DEDICATION

This book is dedicated in loving memory to Stanley A. Rose,
who always taught me that I could be
whatever I wanted to be when I grew up.

ABOUT FIFO:

Fifo is a brown bear from Denali National Park. He is six years old, and in the first grade. Today is the first day of school, and Fifo is a bit scared. Mama comforts him with his favorite breakfast, and they talk about what he wants to be when he grows up. By the end of breakfast, Fifo's been a doctor, a fireman, a pilot, a policeman, a teacher and even the president. Now he's ready for anything, even the first day of school.

This is Fifo, he is such a good bear.
He is six years old, and has brown fluffy hair.

"Fifo," Mama shouts, "get up and come downstairs."
You see it is the first day of school and Fifo's a bit scared.

So Fifo gets up and brushes his teeth.
He runs downstairs and takes his seat.

"For this special day," Mama smiled, "I have made you a treat.
What is warm and squishy, and really fun to eat?"

"Yummy oatmeal," Fifo laughed, "my favorite!"

"Fifo," Mama says, "you are smart, we can see.
So when you grow up, what do you want to be?"

"I want to be a Doctor," Fifo said.
"When your tummy hurts, or there is a pain in your head . . .

You can come to me and I will make you feel better.
A doctor's job is to heal the sick, when they are feeling under the weather."

"Or maybe a Fireman," Fifo said.
"I will ride a red fire engine to the fires and then . . .

I will hook up the hoses and pump the water.
I will put out those fires that burn even hotter."

"I know, I will be a Pilot," Fifo said.
"I will fly high in the sky through the clouds and then . . .

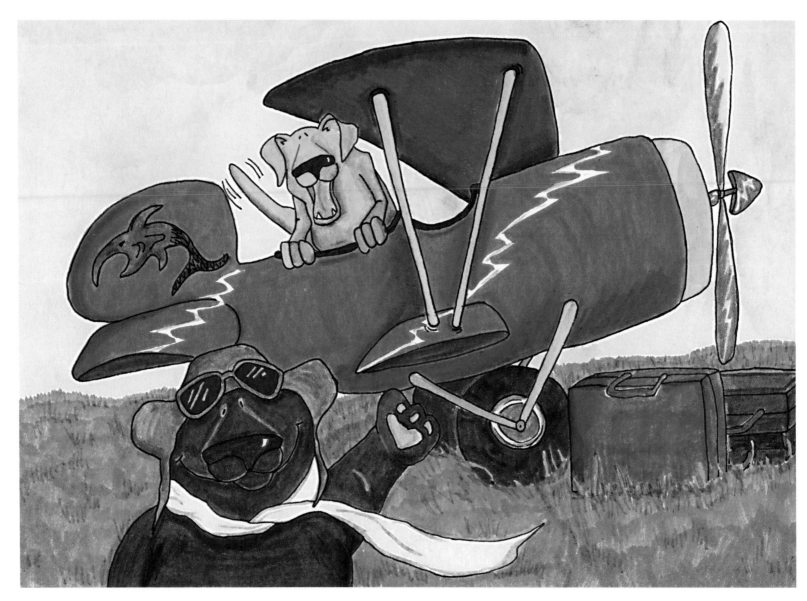

I will fly all of my passengers to all different places,
to visit their families, round the world on vacations."

"I think I will be a Policeman," Fifo said.
"I will watch all the traffic go by and when . . .

I see someone out there breaking the law,
I will give them a ticket from my patrol car."

"Mama, could I be a Teacher," Fifo asked?
"I could teach reading and science and have my own class.

Then we would all go to lunch, we would play, dance and sing.
Then it's back to learn math, art and history."

Then Fifo thought for a moment,
as he puffed out his chest.

"Maybe I could be the President of the United States.
Wow, that would be the best!"

"Well Mama," Fifo laughed, "what ever I choose to be,
I will do my best and you will be proud of me."

Mama smiled and said,
as she patted Fifo's head,

"You have got a good mind. You have got a good heart.
You are going to school, and that's a good start."

"Now don't be late on your very first day.
And Fifo my little bear, you are on your way."

ABOUT THE AUTHOR:

Hayley Rose was born in Los Angeles, CA. In the early 90's she traveled the U.S. with her band Crush Violet. As a singer/songwriter, she has worked and recorded songs with members of Supertramp and the Cutting Crew. After moving to Arizona in 1995, she continued music and branched out into childrens books. Currently she is working on an entire series of Fifo books.

Hayley lives in Scottsdale with her cat Fraidy.

ABOUT THE ILLUSTRATOR:

Jessie Orlet grew up surrounded by artists and animals. She and her husband, James, are always on the road. They pack up their two dogs, Boomer and Trig, and live out of the back of their truck in such amazing places as Arizona, California, Colorado and Alaska. In an attempt to chronicle their many adventures, she began illustrating them and in the process stumbled upon her artistic style.